Be * a * Gem *

Let Your Goodness Shine

by Nancy Steyer Stapleton

Illustrations by Megan D. Wellman

FERNE PRESS

Be a Gem: Let Your Goodness Shine

Copyright © 2012 by Nancy Steyer Stapleton

Layout and cover design by Susan Leonard
Illustrations by Megan D. Wellman
Illustrations created with colored pencils, markers, and watercolors.

Printed in the United States of America

Summary: Meet a group of girls making good choices and learn about different types of gems.

Library of Congress Cataloging-in-Publication Data
Stephenson, Nancy Steyer
Be a Gem: Let Your Goodness Shine/Nancy Steyer Stapleton–First Edition
ISBN-13: 978-1-933916-96-5
1. Juvenile fiction. 2. Values. 3. Self-esteem. 4. Lessons. 5. Making good choices.
I. Stephenson, Nancy Steyer II. Title
Library of Congress Control Number: 2012933010

FERNE PRESS

Ferne Press is an imprint of Nelson Publishing & Marketing
366 Welch Road, Northville, MI 48167
www.nelsonpublishingandmarketing.com
(248) 735-0418

This book is dedicated to the two "gems" in my life,
my daughters, Katey and Carey.
Thanks and love to my mom, Margo,
for her love and support.
And kudos to my friend Laurie
for her helping hand.

Ruby, Ruby, walk the dog,
brush the cat, and feed the frog.
These are things you can't forget
when you're the owner of a pet.

Animals need loving care.
Fill their bowls and wash their hair.
Fed and clean, they'll love you so,
lick your face or nibble your toe!

Sparkle Fact:
In Asia, rubies were laid under buildings to bring good luck to those inside.
They also were used to ornament the armor of noblemen and the
harnesses of their horses.

Beryl, Beryl, please don't litter.
It makes people very bitter!
No one likes to look at junk,
slimy slime, or gooey gunk!

Collect your glass, plastic, and tins,
and put them in recycle bins.
Help our Earth stay safe and clean.
That's what's known as "being green"!

PLASTIC

CANS

GLASS

Sparkle Fact:
Beryl is formed from precious crystals in the center of the Earth.
It comes in many magnificent colors, but beryl can also be colorless.
In ancient times, beryl was used to make eyeglasses.

Amber, Amber, why so sad?
Thinking about the fight you had?
Say you're sorry to your friend.
Now the friendship's on the mend.

You know when someone's mean to you,
it hurts your feelings and makes you blue.
It's better to be nice and kind,
then many friendships you will find.

Sparkle Fact:
Millions of people learned from the movie Jurassic Park that amber, which is fossilized pine tree resin, can hold dinosaur DNA.

Sapphire, Sapphire, it's nice to share
It shows people that you care.
Don't be bossy, mean, or cruel,
during play, at home, or school.

Lend a toy, a book, or game,
then your friend will do the same.
Share your time and share your space.
Share the smile upon your face.

Sparkle Fact:
Women in many countries wish for a sapphire for their engagement ring because it symbolizes loyalty and harmony.

Jade, Jade, don't be afraid.
Come and try to rollerblade!
There's lots of things that you should try.
Attempt just one. Don't be shy!

Try to sing, paint, or dance.
Learn to swim. Just take a chance!
You'll never know what you can do,
unless you dare to see it through.

Sparkle Fact:
In prehistoric times, jade was used to make weapons and tools because of its toughness. Today it is used primarily in jewelry and sculptures.

Aggie, Aggie, please ride safely.
Use your helmet for your safety.
Look both ways to cross the street.
Use your light when shadows creep.

Make sure your bike's in good repair;
chain is greased and tires have air.
Watch for holes along the way,
and you'll keep riding every day!

Sparkle Fact:
Most of the world's agates were developed in volcanic lava. In ancient times, magicians used agates to divert storms, quench thirst, and protect against fever.

Coral, Coral, mind your manners.
"Please" and "thank you" always matter.
Use a napkin when you're eating.
Say "excuse me" when you're sneezing.

Hold the door for those not able.
Keep your elbows off the table.
Being polite and never rude,
changes people's attitude!

Sparkle Fact:

Coral grows underwater, just like pearls. In some cultures, red coral is worn around the neck to protect the wearer against evil spirits.

Crystal, Crystal, please don't yell.
We can hear you very well.
Keep low your voice in certain spaces,
like churches, schools, and other places.

MEDIA CENTER

When picking out a book to read,
quiet voices are a must indeed!
Visit a hospital when someone's ill.
Speaking softly fits the bill.

Sparkle Fact:

Crystals are thought to supply strength and energy.
They come in a variety of colors, shapes, and sizes.

Opal, Opal, what'd you do?
Your room's a mess and so are you!
Clean this mess up, don't delay,
then you may go out to play.

Hang your clothes up so they're neat.
Dirty socks should leave your feet!
Make your bed and change your shirt.
Dust and vacuum all the dirt.

Sparkle Fact:

Opals are the national gemstone of Australia. Almost 95 percent of all fine opals come from the dry and remote outback desert of that country.

Pearl, Pearl, why so late?
Your mother said be home by eight!
Hurry, hurry, get home fast!
Your mother worries when time has passed.

Remember when your dad was tardy
to take you to the birthday party?
It made you mad to sit and wait,
so watch the clock. You won't be late.

Sparkle Fact:
Pearls are formed underwater inside oyster or mussel shells. Natural pearls can be distinguished from imitation ones by rubbing them gently against the tooth. Natural pearls will feel rough and imitation pearls will feel smooth.

Emmy, Emmy, you've got to learn.
When I'm talking, wait your turn.
I'll let you know when I am done.
Then we can talk one on one.

If you want to ask permission
to watch TV or go out fishin',
or have a friend come to play,
I'll let you know if it's okay.

Sparkle Fact:
The Inca and Aztec people of South America regarded the emerald
as a holy gemstone that promised good luck.

Goldie, Goldie, win the game!
But if you lose, don't place the blame.
Everyone plays the best they're able,
on the field or at the table.

If you lose or even tie,
please don't groan, moan, or cry.
Your turn to win will come one day.
That's why the game is fun to play!

Sparkle Fact:
India buys and sells 400 to 800 tons of gold every year
for jewelry making.

The Jewelry Box Girls have done their best
to do their chores and all the rest.
They hope that you will be a "gem"
and do these things as well as them!

List of Things to Do:

 Ruby .... Care for Pets

 Beryl .... Don't Litter, Do Recycle

 Amber .... Get Along With Others

 Sapphire .... Share

 Jade .... Try New Things

 Aggie .... Ride Bike Safely

 Coral .... Be Polite

More Things to Do:

 Crystal ....Watch Voice Volume

 Opal ....Clean Room and Self

 Pearl ....Be on Time

 Emmy ....Don't Interrupt

 Goldie ....Do Your Best

You!.........All of the Above

Birthstones

January .... Garnet	July .... Ruby
February .... Amethyst	August .... Peridot
March .... Aquamarine	September .... Sapphire
April .... Diamond	October .... Opal
May .... Emerald	November .... Topaz
June .... Pearl	December .... Turquoise

Types of Jewelry

Rings: fingers and toes

Bracelets: wrists and ankles (ID bracelets, charm bracelets)

Necklaces: lariats, pendants, chokers

Pins and brooches: hats and lapels

Earrings: pierced, studs, hoops, dangles, clips

About The Author

Nancy Steyer Stapleton is a first-time children's book author. Born and raised in Grosse Pointe, Michigan, she now resides in St. Clair Shores, Michigan with her two daughters and Malti-Tzu, Misty. Nancy hand paints furniture and interiors of homes, and in her spare time enjoys gardening, reading, and watching her beloved Red Wings. For more information about Nancy, please visit her on Facebook at www.facebook.com/NancyStapletonBooks.

About The Illustrator

Megan D. Wellman grew up in Redford, Michigan, and currently resides with her husband, Brent, daughter, Kylee, two Great Danes, and a cat in Canton, Michigan. She holds a bachelor's degree in fine arts from Eastern Michigan University with a minor in children's theater. *Be a Gem* is Megan's thirteenth book. Her books include *Stella, Our Star: Coping with a Loss during Pregnancy*, *My Guy in the Sky*, *Halle and Tiger with their Bucketfilling Family*, *Does This Make Me Beautiful?*, *Liam's Luck and Finnegan's Fortune*, *King of Dilly Dally*, *This Babe So Small*, *Lonely Teddy*, *Grandma's Ready*, *...and that is why we teach*, *Being Bella*, and *Read to Me, Daddy!* which are all available from Ferne Press.